Dear Parents,

Welcome to the Scholastic Reader serie
years of experience with teachers, parer
it into a program that is designed to ma
and skills.

Level 1—Short sentences and stories made up of words kids
can sound out using their phonics skills and words that are
important to remember.

Level 2—Longer sentences and stories with words kids need
to know and new "big" words that they will want to know.

Level 3—From sentences to paragraphs to longer stories, these
books have large "chunks" of texts and are made up of a rich
vocabulary.

Level 4—First chapter books with more words and fewer
pictures.

It is important that children learn to read well enough to succeed
in school and beyond. Here are ideas for reading this book with
your child:

- Look at the book together. Encourage your child to read the
  title and make a prediction about the story.
- Read the book together. Encourage your child to sound out
  words when appropriate. When your child struggles, you can
  help by providing the word.
- Encourage your child to retell the story. This is a great way
  to check for comprehension.
- Have your child take the fluency test on the last page to check
  progress.

Scholastic Readers are designed to support your child's efforts
to learn how to read at every age and every stage. Enjoy
helping your child learn to read and love to read.

—Francie Alexander
Chief Education Officer
Scholastic Education

For Cassie
R.I.

For Deli
K.M.

Text copyright © 2003 by Rose Impey.
Illustrations copyright © 2003 by Katharine McEwen.
Originally published in the UK in 2003 under the title *Titchy Witch and the Stray Dragon* by Orchard Books UK.

Published by Scholastic Inc.
SCHOLASTIC, CARTWHEEL BOOKS, and associated logos are trademarks and/or registered trademarks of Scholastic Inc.

ISBN 0-439-78452-2

10 9 8 7 6 5   07 08 09 10

Printed in the U.S.A.   23
First Scholastic printing, September 2006

Wanda Witch
and the Stray Dragon

Rose Impey ★ Katharine McEwen

Scholastic Reader — Level 3

SCHOLASTIC INC.

New York Toronto London Auckland Sydney
Mexico City New Delhi Hong Kong Buenos Aires

Wanda Witch *really* wanted a pet.
But Witchy Witch said,
"I'm sorry, my little charmer."

"There are too many pets in this
house already," said Cat-a-bogus.

Cat-a-bogus wasn't a pet.
He was Witchy Witch's magic
cat, and he thought he was
the boss of the house!

Victor wasn't *much* of a pet.
He was too old and sleepy.

And Eric wasn't friendly at all.

Anyway, Wanda Witch wanted
a pet of her own.
So she tried to magic one.

"Scales, skin, feather, fur.
Hiss, growl, woof, purr.
Don't care what I get.
Just bring me a pet!"

Luckily her spells didn't
last very
long.

One morning, Wanda Witch heard
a noise outside.

It was love at first sight.

The baby dragon put his head
in her lap.

"Oh, no," said Cat-a-bogus.
"No, no, no, no, no."

When Mom and Dad came
home, they said "no," too.

But he's
so cute!

"He won't be cute when he's grown," said Witchy Witch. "He'll roar his head off."
"And breathe fire everywhere," said Wendel.

They led the baby dragon outside.
"Go and find your mommy."

But the next morning, the baby
dragon was still there, looking
up at the door hopefully.

So they took him to the Dragon
Rescue Center.

But it's
so sad!

When they saw all the baby
dragons with no homes to go to,
they couldn't bear to leave him.

"You can keep him while he's
a baby," said Mom and Dad,
"but when he's bigger than you…
he has to go!"
"Superdoodle!" squealed
Wanda Witch.

I shall call
him Dido!

Dido slept in a basket by her bed,
or sometimes on the end of it.

Wanda Witch and Dido went
everywhere together.
He even went with her
to school, at least as far
as the gates.

At home, the little dragon helped Wanda Witch with her homework.

And sometimes her spells!

Wanda Witch was very happy, and
so was Dido.

But then he started to grow.

Soon he was
almost as tall
as she was.

Wanda Witch decided that if Dido
had to go, she would go, too.
She decided to fly away.

When everyone was asleep,
Wanda Witch and Dido
crept downstairs.

But the little dragon was so heavy
now, the broomstick
could hardly take off.

It kept crash-landing.
In the end, they woke
Cat-a-bogus!

"Dido keeps on growing," Wanda Witch explained, "so we're flying away." Cat-a-bogus purred while he thought about this.

The truth was, Dido was very useful in the kitchen. The cat didn't want to lose his little helper.

The next day, Cat-a-bogus helped Wanda Witch make a special shrinking spell.

"Teeny, tiny, weeny, wink. Make this little dragon shrink!"

Dido shrank until he was just
the right size.
He didn't mind, as long as he could
stay with Wanda Witch.

"Have you noticed Dido never seems to grow?" said Dad.

"He must be a special small kind of dragon," said Mom.

Wanda Witch gave Dido
a big hug.

Oh, yes, he was a *special*
dragon all right.

Join the SCHOLASTIC READING CIRCLE—
children will love to read together, read with
assistance, and read alone!

1 LEVEL
Simple words and short sentences for the newest readers

2 LEVEL
Vocabulary and sentence length for beginning readers

3 LEVEL
Longer stories with paragraphs

4 LEVEL
First chapter books for advanced beginners